This book belongs to

Kayla

I hope you enjoy these six magical stories.

Love,
Auntie Janice

Based on the TV series *Dora the Explorer*® as seen on Nick Jr.®

No part of this publication may be reproduced, or stored in a retrieval system,
or transmitted in any form or by any means, electronic, mechanical, photocopying,
recording, or otherwise, without written permission of the publisher. For information
regarding permission, write to Simon Spotlight, Simon & Schuster Children's
Publishing Division, 1230 Avenue of the Americas, New York, NY 10020.

ISBN 0-439-66665-1

Copyright © 2004 by Viacom International Inc. NICKELODEON, NICK JR.,
Dora the Explorer, and all related titles, logos, and characters are registered
trademarks of Viacom International Inc. All rights reserved. Published by Scholastic Inc.,
557 Broadway, New York, NY 10012, by arrangement with Simon Spotlight,
Simon & Schuster Children's Publishing Division. SCHOLASTIC and associated
logos are trademarks and/or registered trademarks of Scholastic Inc.

12 11 10 9 8 7 6 5 4 3 2 1   4 5 6 7 8 9/0

Printed in the U.S.A.

First Scholastic printing, November 2004

NICK JR.

DORA'S Favorite FAIRY TALES

adapted by Leslie Goldman • illustrated by A&J Studios

SCHOLASTIC INC.

New York Toronto London Auckland Sydney
Mexico City New Delhi Hong Kong Buenos Aires

¡Hola! Boots and I are at the gate to Fairy-Tale Land. Do you want to come inside with us? To open the gate you just have to say "Once upon a time!"

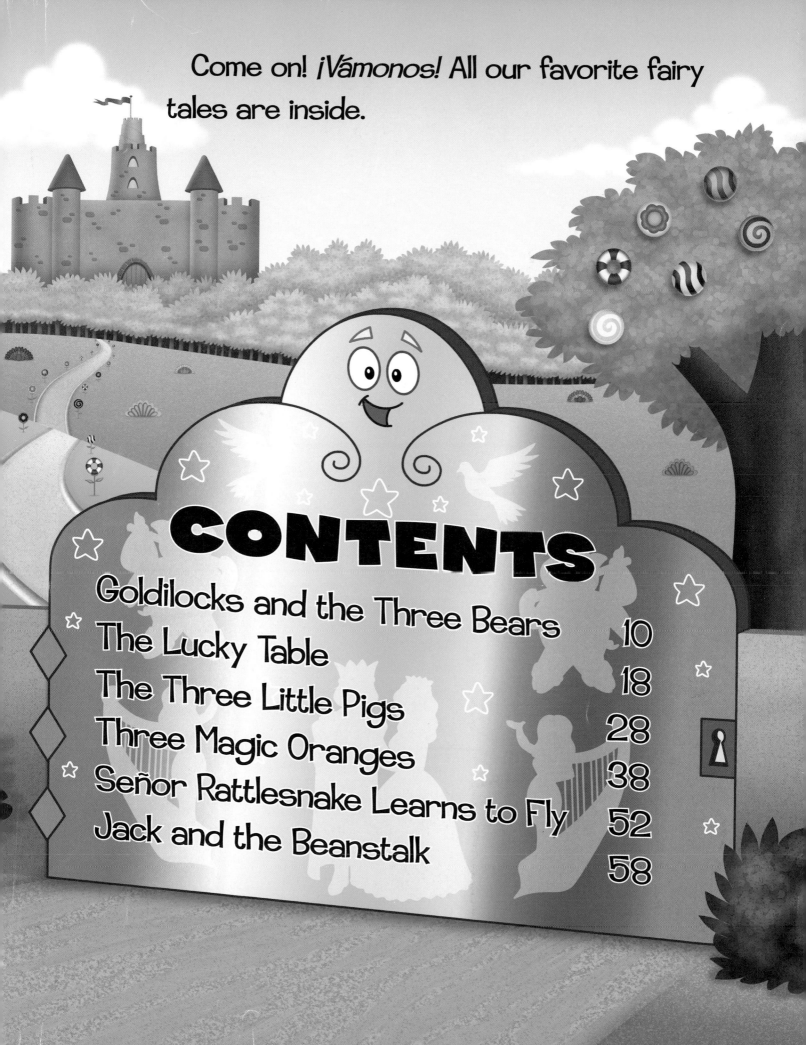

Come on! ¡Vámonos! All our favorite fairy tales are inside.

CONTENTS

GOLDILOCKS AND THE THREE BEARS

Once upon a time there were three bears: Mamá Osa, Papá Oso, and Bebé Osito. They all lived together in a house in the woods.

Bebé Osito was small, so he had a small bowl for porridge. Mamá Osa was medium-sized, so she had a medium-sized bowl for porridge. And since Papá Oso was such a great big bear, he had a great big bowl.

In the living room each of the three bears had their very own chair to sit in. Bebé Osito's chair was small. Mamá Osa's chair was medium, and Papá Oso's chair was large.

All three bears had their own beds, too. As you may have already guessed, Bebé Osito's bed was tiny. Mamá Osa's bed was medium-sized, and Papá Oso's bed was extra large.

One morning the bears made some porridge, but it was too hot to eat right away.

"Let's go for a walk in the woods," said Mamá Osa. "By the time we get back, the porridge will be cool."

"Okay," said Papá Oso. "That sounds like a fine idea."

"Yippee!" said Bebé Osito, who loved to go on walks in the woods. He skipped outside, and his parents followed close behind.

While they were out, a young girl named Goldilocks stumbled upon the house. She'd been walking in the woods for a very long time and was tired and hungry. When she knocked on the door no one answered. She peeked through the window, but no one seemed to be home. Sniffing the air, she smelled something delicious—porridge! Since her stomach was growling, and porridge happened to be her favorite food, Goldilocks opened the door and walked right into the house.

Goldilocks went to the kitchen and saw three bowls on the counter. First she tasted the porridge from the largest bowl.

"This porridge is too hot," she said. She moved on to the second bowl. "This porridge is too cold." Next she tried the third, smallest bowl. Grinning happily, Goldilocks said, "This porridge is just right." And she gobbled it all up.

After she finished the porridge, Goldilocks wanted to sit down. Walking into the living room, she saw three chairs. Goldilocks sat in the first chair. It was Papá Oso's. "This chair is too big!" she exclaimed, jumping up out of the chair.

She sat down in Mamá Osa's chair next but not for very long. "This chair is too big too," she said.

Next she sat in the third, smallest chair. It was Bebé Osito's. "This chair is just right!" said Goldilocks. But suddenly there was a strange creaking noise, and the chair broke.

"Ouch!" said Goldilocks as she fell to the ground. Picking herself up, she suddenly felt very sleepy. She went upstairs to the bedroom

and lay down on the first bed. "This bed is too hard," she said. Trying out the second bed, she said, "This bed is too soft!" Lucky for her there was still one bed left to try. "This bed is just right!" she said with a sleepy sigh. Goldilocks closed her eyes and yawned. Soon she fell asleep.

Meanwhile the bears finished up their walk in the woods. "I'm so hungry," said Bebé Osito.

"Me too," said Mamá Osa. "I'll bet the porridge is cool by now. We should go home."

When they reached their house Papá Oso said, "That's funny. I don't remember leaving the front door wide open!"

Rushing to the kitchen, Papá Oso growled, "Someone's been eating my porridge!"

Mamá Osa looked down at her own bowl and gasped, "Someone's been eating my porridge too!"

Bebé Osito peered into his bowl. "Someone's been eating my porridge and has eaten it all up!" he cried.

Papá Oso hurried into the living room. "Someone's been sitting in my chair!" he bellowed.

"Someone's been sitting in my chair too!" Mamá Osa exclaimed.

Bebé Osito started to cry as he stared at the mess that used to be his chair. "Someone's been sitting in my chair and has broken it!"

Mamá Osa and Papá Oso gave Bebé Osito a hug. When he was feeling better they went upstairs to the bedroom.

Papá Oso growled, "Someone's been sleeping in my bed!"

"Someone's been sleeping in my bed too!" cried Mamá Osa.

"Someone's been sleeping in my bed," said Bebé Osito, pointing to the sleeping girl. "And she's still there!"

Suddenly Goldilocks woke up. Seeing the three bears standing over her, she let out a scream. Then she jumped up and ran out of the room.

Down the stairs and out the door Goldilocks ran. She ran through the woods and never returned to the home of the three bears.

And once the three bears made a new batch of porridge, built Bebé Osito a new chair, and put a lock on their door, they lived happily ever after.

THE LUCKY TABLE

Once upon a time there was a widow who lived with her two sons. Her oldest son, a sensible boy, was named Pedro. Her younger son was named Bobo because he was very, very silly. Bobo didn't understand the value of money and would spend it on useless things. He was just as bad when he wanted to sell something. He would take whatever price was offered—even if it was very, very low.

The widow and her sons were poor, but they never went hungry. One year, however, things got very bad. Their small patch of corn dried up, so they had no corn to make tortillas. Their bean vines shriveled, so they had no black beans to eat with their rice. Their goat ran away and could not be found, and then their hens would not lay eggs. All that they had left was their cow.

"Take the cow to the market and sell her," said the widow to her two sons. "But make sure you get the very best price."

"Don't worry, Mamá," said Bobo. "We'll sell her and we'll get a lot of money for her."

The next day Pedro and Bobo said good-bye to their mother and went to the marketplace, leading their cow behind them on a rope. They walked and walked, uphill and then downhill. They met many people who were also traveling to the marketplace. Some pulled coffee beans in oxcarts. Some traveled with chickens or pigs, and some were bringing bananas and sweet cakes to the market.

When they reached the market Pedro had another errand to do for his mother. He left the cow with Bobo, saying, "I'll be right back. Don't sell the cow without me."

"Of course not," said Bobo.

When Pedro went away, Bobo sat down under a tree to rest in the shade.

Soon a boy walked by. He was carrying a wooden table on his head. "¡Buenas tardes!" he said to Bobo.

"¡Buenas tardes!" Bobo replied.

"What do you plan to do with that cow?" asked the boy, who had heard all about Bobo.

"I plan to sell her," said Bobo. "But I have to wait until my older brother gets back."

"Don't sell her." The boy put the table down on the ground. "You'll do better to trade her."

"Trade her?" asked Bobo.

"Yes," said the boy. "It's obvious that the cow is a sorry beast. She is old and skinny. I'm sure she's hardly worth the cost it would take to feed her."

Bobo looked at the cow, which was in fact old and skinny. "I think you're right," he said.

"Tell you what," said the boy. "I'll trade you my table for her."

"Done!" said Bobo. "You take the cow and let me have the table."

"Done," the boy said happily. "The table is yours." The boy took hold of the rope and quickly led the cow away.

Bobo smiled and clapped his hands. "My brother will be so happy when I tell him about my wonderful trade," he said to himself.

When Pedro returned and saw Bobo without the cow, he started to worry. Rushing forward, he asked, "Where is the cow? Did you sell her? What did you get for her? And where is the money?"

Bobo smiled at his brother. "Don't you worry," he said. "I haven't sold the cow."

"Oh, good." Pedro looked around the market. "Then where is she?"

"I traded her for this table!"

Pedro was shocked. "What?" he asked. "You traded her for a table? Why? Mamá told us to sell the cow only for the highest price. Now what will we do? I never thought you'd be so silly as to trade our wonderful cow for a simple table, Bobo!" Then Pedro dropped to his knees and started to weep.

"This is a great table," said Bobo. "The cow was old and skinny. The boy even said so. We were very lucky to get the table."

Seeing that there was no point in trying to reason with his silly brother, Pedro dried his tears and stood. "We may as well go home," he said.

"Okay," said Bobo, who couldn't understand why Pedro was so upset.

Before they left, Pedro said, "Since you made the trade, you can carry the table home by yourself."

Bobo lifted the table up onto his head. Since it was so heavy, he wasn't able to walk very fast.

Hours later they arrived at a dark forest. Hearing the night birds starting to chirp, the brothers realized it would soon grow dark.

The path was empty. There was not an oxcart or another person in sight. Since the forest ahead looked dark and scary, they decided to spend the night where they were.

"We should climb up there," said Pedro, pointing to a tall tree with wide branches. "Otherwise the prowling pumas might find us!"

Fearing that the table would be stolen, they took it with them. Bobo carried it on his head, and it wasn't easy. The table was heavy.

Once they settled themselves in the branches, they heard some men's voices.

"Someone's coming," said Bobo.

"Shh!" Pedro said. "Be quiet. They could be robbers. If they see us, they might hurt us."

Pedro and Bobo watched as the men sat down beneath the tree, right below them. It seemed that they were in fact robbers because as soon as they sat down, they began to count out a large pile of gold pieces.

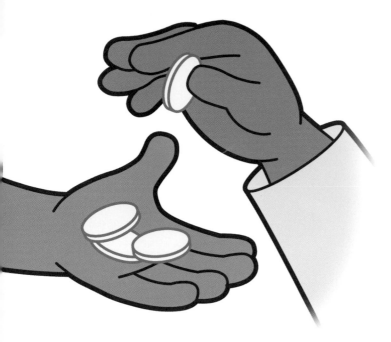

"Ten for Paco, ten for Hector," said one of the robbers. "And ten for Esteban." They continued counting for a long time.

Bobo, who still had the table on his head, began to get very tired. "Brother," he whispered. "I can't hold on to this table for much longer. It's hurting my head."

"Shh!" said Pedro. "They're going to hear you."

"I can't help it," Bobo cried in a low voice. "It's too heavy, and I must drop it."

"But they'll find us," said Pedro, who was very worried.

Bobo tried to stay still and silent, but the weight was too much. The table started to slip. "Pedro," he said. "I cannot hold the table much longer."

"You must," Pedro whispered.

"It's slipping!" cried Bobo.

"If you let it fall," said Pedro, "that will be the end of us!"

But Bobo had no choice. "*¡Ay!*" he shouted, as the table slipped off his head and went tumbling down. Down and down it went, breaking branches along the way.

With a terrible crash it landed right in the middle of the robbers.

Pedro closed his eyes, terrified that the robbers would spot them.

But the robbers were so scared by the table falling from the sky that they ran away, leaving behind all of their treasure.

Pedro and Bobo climbed down the tree. They gathered the treasure and carried it home, together with the lucky table.

When they returned home their mother was so pleased! They had a big feast and never went hungry again. And everyone had to admit that maybe Bobo wasn't so silly after all!

THE THREE LITTLE PIGS

Once upon a time there was a mother pig who lived with her three little pigs. When they grew up, the three little pigs wanted to build houses of their own. "Be careful that the wolf doesn't catch you," their mother warned.

"We will!" they said, as they kissed and hugged their mother good-bye.

"Don't forget to write!" she called to them.

Soon after the pigs had begun their journey, they met a bull who was pushing a large wheelbarrow filled with straw.

"Please give me some straw," said the first little pig. "I want to build a house for myself."

"Here you go," said the bull. He handed the first little pig enough straw for a one-room house.

It took just a few hours for the first little pig to build his house. And he was very pleased when he was finished.

"Now the wolf won't catch me," he said, settling into his new chair, which was also made of straw.

"I will build a stronger house than yours," said the second little pig.

"I will build a stronger house than yours too," said the third little pig.

"Okay," said the first little pig, who didn't care about having a strong house. All he wanted to do was take a nap. As the second little pig and the third little pig continued on their way, the first little pig called, "Don't forget to write!"

The second and third little pigs soon met a beaver who was carrying some sticks on his back.

"Please give me some sticks," said the second little pig. "I want to build a house for myself."

"Okay," said the beaver,

handing the second little pig enough sticks for a one-room house.

The house of sticks was much stronger than the house of straw, and the second little pig was very pleased with himself. "Now the wolf won't catch me," he said, settling into his chair, which was also made of sticks.

The third little pig frowned at his brother. "I will build a stronger house than yours," he said.

"Okay," said the second little pig, who thought that his house was strong enough. "Don't forget to write."

The third little pig walked along. When he met a duck with a load of bricks, he asked, "Please, will you give me some bricks? I want to build a house for myself."

"Yes, gladly," said the duck. And he gave the third little pig enough bricks for a one-room house.

The third little pig built a very strong house for himself. It took him a long time, but when he finished he was very happy. "Now the wolf won't catch me," he said, settling down into his chair, which was also made of bricks.

The next day when the wolf was prowling he noticed the house of straw.

The first little pig saw the wolf coming, and he ran inside and shut the door. Moments later he heard a sharp knock.

"Little pig, little pig, let me come in!" said the wolf.

"No, no," said the pig. "I won't let you in. Not by the hair of my chinny, chin, chin."

"Then I'll huff and I'll puff and I'll blow your house in," said the wolf. He huffed and he puffed, and soon the house of straw fell down.

"Ahh!" the little pig squealed, and he ran to his brother's house of sticks.

The wolf followed close behind. It wasn't long before he knocked on the door of the house of sticks and said, "Little pigs, little pigs, let me come in!"

"No, no," said the first and second little pigs. "We won't let you in. Not by the hair of our chinny, chin, chins."

"I'll huff and I'll puff and I'll blow your house in," said the wolf. He huffed and he puffed, and he huffed and puffed some more. He had to work very hard, but eventually he managed to blow the house of sticks in.

"Ahh!" the two pigs squealed, and they ran to their brother's house of bricks.

The wolf followed close behind. It wasn't long before he knocked on the door of the house of bricks and said, "Little pigs, little pigs, let me come in!"

"No, no," said all three little pigs. "We won't let you in. Not by the hair of our chinny, chin, chins."

"Then I'll huff and I'll puff and I'll blow your house in," said the

wolf. He huffed and he puffed, and he huffed and puffed some more.

But the house would not budge.

"I'll get you," said the wolf, as he circled the house. When he found the chimney he started to climb.

Meanwhile the first and the second little pigs were frozen with fear. But the third little pig quickly started a fire.

The wolf felt his tail getting hotter and hotter as he began to climb down the chimney. Then he saw the flames! So he scrambled back up the chimney, ran into the woods, and never bothered the three little pigs ever again.

The next day the three little pigs sat down and wrote a letter:

Dear Mom,
WE'VE MOVED!
From now on, you can write to us all at the house of bricks.

Love,
your
Three Little Pigs

THREE MAGIC ORANGES

In the olden days there lived a king who had a son. Since the king was getting old, he wanted his son to get married. He held a great fiesta, inviting all of the beautiful, smart, and talented princesses from far and near. But the prince was in no hurry to find a wife. He found something wrong with each of the princesses at the fiesta. One was too tall and one was too short. One was too old and one was too young. One of them spoke so softly that the prince had trouble hearing her, and one spoke so loudly that she gave the prince a headache.

The king was not happy. He ordered his son to go out at once and find a wife. "If you ever want to wear a crown on your head, you will not return without a bride!"

The prince found a fine horse and rode out into the world alone in search of a wife. Soon he came to a green forest. At the edge of it he saw an orange tree with three golden oranges.

The prince plucked the magnificent-looking fruits and continued to ride. He rode on and on and on.

The sun beat down in the cloudless sky. The prince grew terribly thirsty, but there was not a stream or a spring in sight. Then he remembered the oranges. He pulled one from his pocket and held it up. It was so bright and golden. He imagined it to be full of sweet juice. His mouth watered and his lips cooled just thinking about the refreshing taste. The prince hopped off his horse, sat down, and cut the orange in half.

As soon as the prince cut open the orange, a beautiful maiden appeared before him. She had eyes as blue as the sky and hair as golden yellow as the sun. She begged him for a drink of water. "At the very least, a drop," she said.

"I cannot give you what I do not have," the prince said, sadly.

As quickly as she had appeared, the beautiful maiden vanished.

The prince stared at the place where she'd been standing. Stroking his chin, he said to himself, "Well, now that I know what sort of oranges these are, I'll be careful when I open them."

He ate the orange quickly. He had never tasted anything so sweet and delicious, and when he was done he even licked his fingers. Feeling refreshed, the prince continued on his way.

However it did not take long for his mouth to become dry again, and soon he was thirsty. Since there was still no water in sight, and his thirst was stronger than his good sense, the prince pulled the second orange from his pocket.

When he cut into it, the same thing happened all over again. But this time the maiden's eyes were green, like a pool of water. And her hair was flaming red, like a hibiscus flower. "Please, may I have some water?" she begged. "Even just a drop."

Hearing that the prince had none to offer, she vanished.

"Well," he said, "I still have one orange. I will not cut it open until I have some water handy."

The prince ate the second orange and continued on his way. Soon after, he heard a faint rippling noise. He galloped toward the sound and was pleased to find a lively spring with water as clear as the air itself.

Jumping off his horse, the prince ran to the spring and drank deeply. Once he was refreshed he sat down to rest on a grassy bank nearby. Then he felt for his third orange. Why, this is the very place to open it! he realized. He did so, and in an instant there appeared before him a maiden. Her eyes and her long flowing hair were as black as a raven's wings, and her face was soft and white, like a jasmine flower. She was so beautiful the prince was momentarily stunned.

Like the others, the maiden asked for water. And not losing one second, the prince scooped up some water in the hollow of his hands and raised it to her lips.

The maiden did not vanish like the others. Rather she drank the water.

The prince could not help noticing that the maiden was neither too tall, nor too short. She was not too old or too young, and her voice was neither too loud nor too soft. In fact it was music to his ears. She was so beautiful and charming that the prince instantly fell in love. He knelt down upon one knee and asked the lovely maiden to become his wife.

"Yes," she said. "Thank you for breaking this cruel curse. You've no idea what it's like to be stuck in an orange for years and years!"

"It must have been horrible," said the prince.

"You know," she said, "I was once a king's daughter, but an evil witch cast a spell upon me and imprisoned me in that magic orange. Only a king's son could break the spell. You are that son, and I am set free!"

Full of joy the prince and princess got onto the prince's horse, and together they rode home to the royal palace.

Once they neared the royal palace they were followed by many cheering people, who threw flowers joyously into the air.

Upon hearing the excitement, the king and all the court came running outside where they met the prince.

"Father, here is the maiden of choice!" the prince shouted happily. The marriage was celebrated with a grand fiesta. Everyone danced and sang and ate and laughed. They had a wonderful time, especially the king whose wish to see his daughter-in-law had finally come true.

Things were quite wonderful.

When they grew older, the prince and the princess became the king and the queen. They wore golden crowns upon their heads. But to say that they lived happily ever after would be to end this story too soon.

Before long, news of the new king and queen reached the witch who had imprisoned the princess inside the magic orange. When the witch found out the princess was not only free, but now a queen, she was very upset. Disguising herself as a poor old woman with a basket full of fruits and fancy pins, she started for the royal palace. When she arrived there she walked up and down the steps shouting, "Fruit! Fruit! I have sweet oranges, bananas, and lemons. Pins! Pins! Please buy my pins!"

Hearing her cries, the queen came to the castle door. The queen did not realize the old woman was really the witch. "Come closer, so I can see some pins," said the queen. The witch walked to the door as quickly as her mean, old, shriveled legs would carry her.

"Here, Queen," she said, picking out a hairpin with a shiny white pearl. "This will look very fine by your golden crown. Do try it on!"

The queen politely bowed down. When the witch placed the pin into her hair, in a flash the lovely queen was turned into a little white dove. Startled, she flew through the open door and vanished into the green forest.

"Ha, ha, ha," the witch cackled. Since her work was done, she returned to her home deep in the woods.

Now all of this had happened while the young king was out hunting in the forest. As he prepared his bow and arrow, he looked up and saw a little white dove on a treetop. The king thought the dove was so beautiful, he immediately wished to capture it as a present for

his wife. He turned and pointed his arrow. It brushed one of the dove's white wings, making her lose her perch and flutter to the ground. He picked her up gently and returned to the castle.

Once there the king placed the dove in a golden cage and carried it to the queen's chamber. But the queen could not be found. "My queen is missing!" shouted the king.

The whole court began to buzz. Up and down everyone searched. But the queen seemed to have vanished from the earth.

Everyone was very sad, especially the king. Day and night he mourned the loss of his wonderful queen. No one could find a way to comfort him.

Two years went by as swiftly as the wind. One day when the unhappy king decided that he needed to be alone, he went into the garden and noticed the beautiful little dove. She had lived in the garden since the queen disappeared.

The king opened the cage door and peered inside. The dove blinked back at him. She was so beautiful, she reminded the king of his wife. Gently the king ran his fingers over the bird's head. As he did, he felt the pearl. Brushing apart the feathers, he discovered the magic hairpin. How strange, the king thought. Why would a bird have such a pin?

Carefully he pulled the pin from the bird's feathers. As soon as he did, the dove vanished, and there before him stood the queen. She was as lovely and as kind as ever. The king fell to his knees in astonishment.

The queen told her husband all about the wicked witch. Immediately the king ordered his men to find the witch and bring her back to the royal palace so that she could be punished.

But there was no need. When the witch's spell was broken for the second time, she lost all of her magical powers and became just a lonely old woman who lived in the woods.

From that day forward the king and his lovely queen truly did live happily ever after.

SEÑOR RATTLESNAKE LEARNS TO FLY

Once upon a time in the desert there lived a rattlesnake named Señor Rattlesnake, who was king of the land, and an eagle named Señor Eagle, who was king of the sky.

For many years the arrangement worked, but over time Señor Rattlesnake grew very jealous. He was tired of slithering across the hot sand on his belly. Being king of the land was good, but he wanted more. Señor Rattlesnake wanted to be the king of both the land and the sky.

Señor Rattlesnake slithered up to two buzzards. "I want to fly through the air like the two of you," he said. "It must feel so wonderful to float so high above the world! I may have the body of a snake, but in my heart I am sure that I am a bird."

Since the buzzards felt sorry for the rattlesnake, they tried to cheer him up. "Flying is okay, *mi amigo*," said the first buzzard. "But so is being on the ground. You can't take a nap when you are in the sky."

"But I want to fly," the snake insisted.

"Everyone fears you on the ground," said the second buzzard. "You rule the land."

Señor Rattlesnake could not be convinced. "It's not enough. I want to see my kingdom from above so that I may rule the sky too."

The buzzards thought long and hard. Finally the first buzzard said, "Although it is impossible for you to fly like a bird, perhaps we can take you for a ride in the sky."

"*Sí, sí!*" said the snake. "Which of you will carry me on your back?"

"Neither of us, *mi amigo*," said the second buzzard. "You are too heavy for just one of us. There has to be another way for both of us to carry you in flight."

"We could do it with a stick!" said the first buzzard. "I'll go find one."

The first buzzard flew off and soon returned with a long, thin yucca stalk. It had dried out in the sun and was both light and strong. Each bird took one end of the stick in his mouth and together they perched on a rock.

"Bite the middle of the stick with your great pointy fangs, *amigo*," said the second buzzard. "And hold on tight!"

Once Señor Rattlesnake had grasped the stick with his fangs, the birds slowly flapped their large black wings. They rose high into the air, carrying the stick and Señor Rattlesnake with them.

The snake gripped the stick tightly with his fangs as his long body swayed in the air. He felt the wind on his tail. Seeing the kingdom from the air was exhilarating. It was better than he had ever imagined!

As Señor Rattlesnake dreamed of conquering the sky, Señor Eagle happened to fly by.

Señor Eagle was very happy being king of the sky. He didn't like seeing his rival in his territory, so he decided to have some fun with the snake. "Why not flap your wings, Señor Rattlesnake? Those are strange feathers growing from your tail. Do you always fly with a stick in your mouth?" he taunted.

Before the snake could respond, a small dove perched right on the yucca stick, very close to Señor Rattlesnake. "Don't be angry, *amigo*," she told him. "Señor Eagle wants you to open your mouth and fall to the ground."

The snake gave the dove an evil look. For a moment he forgot where he was. His true nature took over, and he opened his mouth wide to strike at the eagle.

Down, down, down Señor Rattlesnake fell! He twisted and turned and flew through the air faster than he had ever thought possible. Then he landed in the middle of a prickly pear cactus with a very hard thud!

It took many days for Señor Rattlesnake to recover from his adventures. And with every cactus needle he plucked from his scales, he realized that being the king of the land was quite enough for him.

JACK AND THE BEANSTALK

There once lived a widow who had a son named Jack. They lived in a small house and had one cow. They were so poor that all they had to live on was the milk the cow gave them every morning. Then one day the cow gave no milk.

"It's market day today," said the widow. "We must sell the cow."

Jack said, "Okay, mother." Taking the cow by the halter, he started for the market.

Before he got very far down the path a little funny-looking old man jumped out of the bushes.

"Good afternoon, Jack," he said.

"Good afternoon," said Jack, wondering how the stranger knew his name.

"Where are you going?" asked the little man.

"I'm going to the market," said Jack. "I need to sell our cow."

"Well, I have a better idea," said the stranger. He pulled five beans from his pocket and showed them to Jack. "I'll trade you these five beans for the cow."

Jack started to back away. "That doesn't sound like a very good trade," he said, holding on to the cow's lead very tightly.

"Oh, but it is," said the man. "These beans are magical. If you plant them tonight, by morning they'll grow right up into the sky."

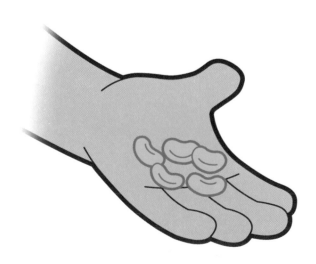

"Really?" asked Jack.

"Yes," said the little man. "It's true."

Jack looked from the cow to the man. After some thought he decided to make the trade. He had never seen magic beans before and was very anxious to see if they worked.

Jack ran home—and he didn't have very far to go.

"Back so soon, Jack?" asked his mother. "I see you haven't got the cow, so you must have sold her. Well done. How much did you get for her?"

"You'll never guess, mother." Jack wore a grin that spread from ear to ear.

His mother beamed down at him. "I see you must have done well! Did you get five gold coins or ten?"

Jack shook his head. His mother's eyes widened. "Did you get fifteen or twenty?" she asked, hopefully.

"No," said Jack. "I told you you'd never guess. Look at these!" He held out his hand to show his mother the beans. "They're magical. Plant them overnight and—"

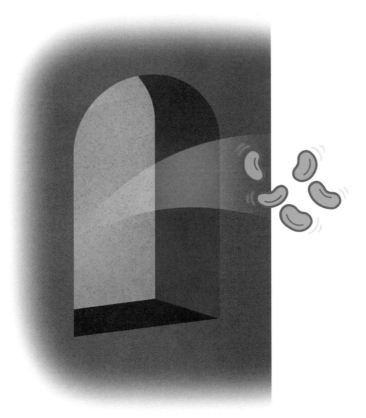

Jack did not get to finish explaining about the beans because his mother started to yell. "What have you done? Are you such a fool? You give away our only cow for five measly beans!" She grabbed the beans from Jack and threw them out the window. "Off to bed!" she yelled. "There will be no supper for you."

Jack climbed upstairs to his little room. He was sad and sorry that his mother was so angry. He was also very, very hungry. After much tossing and turning, Jack dried his tears and fell asleep.

When Jack woke up the next morning he sensed something unusual. His bedroom looked funny. The sun shined into part of it, but the rest of it was strangely dark and shady. Jack jumped up and got dressed. When he went to his window he could hardly believe his eyes.

Outside there was a giant beanstalk growing up into the sky!

The funny little man had spoken the truth. The beans were magical.

Jumping out his bedroom window, Jack grasped a branch on the beanstalk. Looking up, he was even more amazed. The beanstalk had grown higher than the clouds. Jack couldn't even see the end of it! He started to climb up—higher, higher, and higher still. After fifteen minutes of climbing, his arms were tired, but he still hadn't reached the top.

He went past the clouds, and finally the beanstalk started to narrow. Climbing higher, higher, and higher still, he finally made it to the top.

Jack hopped off and found himself on a long, broad road.

He walked along until he came to the biggest house he'd ever seen. On the doorstep was a gigantic woman. "Good day," said Jack, as politely as possible. "Could you please be so kind as to give me some lunch?" Jack hadn't had anything to eat the night before, and he was starving.

"You'd better be careful," said the woman. "My husband is a giant, and he's not very friendly. He'll be coming home soon."

"Please, oh, please," said Jack. "I've never been so hungry."

The giant's wife took pity on Jack. She invited him inside and served him a few slices of cheese, a hunk of bread, and a jug of milk. But Jack wasn't half finished with his lunch when he heard a horrible noise.

Thump! Thump! Thump! With each foot-step, the dishes rattled and the floor shook.

Trembling and wide-eyed, Jack looked up at the woman. "What's that?" he asked in a very small, scared voice.

"It's my husband, *el gigante*," she warned.

"Fee-fi-fo-fum. I smell the smell of a little, little man!" a voice roared.

"Hide, quickly," said the woman. She opened up the oven, and without having time to think, Jack leaped inside.

He couldn't see anything from where he was, but he heard a horrible voice bellow, "Is that a child I smell?"

"A child?" asked the woman. "Why, I don't think so."

El gigante sniffed and looked around.

"There is no child here," said the woman. "Sit down. I'll make you your lunch."

Still grumbling, *el gigante* sat down. When he did, the entire house shuddered. After setting down two enormous satchels, he ate enough food for ten men.

When *el gigante* was through eating, he opened up his satchels. They were filled with gigantic pieces of gold, which he counted and separated into large stacks. Once he finished he started counting all over again until he fell asleep.

El gigante let go a thundering snore, which echoed throughout the house. When the woman left the room Jack sneaked out of the oven. Seeing the gold pieces on the table, he quickly grabbed a few. Jack was sorry to take the gold, but since he and his mother were so poor, and there was so much gold, Jack hoped *el gigante* wouldn't miss a few pieces.

Jack's heart beat faster and faster, not just because he was afraid of *el gigante*, but also because he was starting to get excited. If he made it home, he and his mother would never go hungry again!

Jack tiptoed past *el gigante* and out of the house. Then he ran to the beanstalk and climbed down and down all the way home. He told his mother about *el gigante* and showed her the gold. "See, mother. Wasn't I right about the beans? They really are magical."

Jack's mother happily agreed. And they lived on the gold pieces for some time. When they'd used them all up, Jack decided to try his luck once more. He woke up early one morning and climbed and climbed all the way to the very top of the beanstalk.

He came to the same long, broad road and walked along it. When he reached the enormous house, the giant woman was standing on the doorstep as she had been before.

"Good day, ma'am," said Jack. "Do you think I could have something to eat? I'm very hungry."

"Go away, my boy," said the giant woman. "Or else *el gigante* will be very mad. And aren't you the boy who came here before? Do you know that very day my husband was missing some of his gold?"

"That's strange, ma'am," said Jack. "But I'm too weak with hunger to speak anymore until I've had something to eat."

The giant woman let Jack into her house for a second time. She took him to the kitchen and gave him a few slices of cheese, a hunk of bread, and a jug of milk. But Jack had scarcely begun to eat when his lunch was interrupted.

Thump! Thump! Thump! The sound was so loud it made Jack shake in his boots.

The giant woman opened up the oven and Jack flew inside.

Moments later *el gigante* walked into the room. "Fee-fi-fo-fum! I smell the smell of a little, little man," he bellowed.

"I don't know what you are talking about," said his wife.

El gigante just grunted and sat down to a lunch with enough food for ten men. After lunch he grunted, "Wife, bring me the hen that lays *huevos dorados.*"

Moments later she set the hen down on the table in front of *el gigante.*

When Jack spied the hen his eyes widened, for the hen looked so sad and scared she was shaking.

El gigante shouted, "Lay!" And the hen laid a golden egg!

"Lay, lay, lay!" *el gigante* demanded. He wouldn't let up, and the poor hen had to continue laying egg after egg.

Nodding his head, *el gigante* yawned a great big yawn, and then he fell asleep. Like the last time, the entire house shook with his snores.

Jack crept out of the oven and started to tiptoe toward the door. But the sad little hen caught his eye. Poor thing, I'd better save you! Jack thought. Quick as a wink he grabbed the hen and was off hurrying toward the front door. But as he opened the door it gave a loud creak, waking *el gigante*.

Just as Jack got out of the house he heard *el gigante* call, "Wife, wife, what have you done with my hen?"

And the wife said, "Why, my dear, I've no idea what you mean."

Jack raced off to the beanstalk as fast as his little legs would carry him. He scrambled down the stalk as quickly as he could with the hen tucked under his arm. When he got home he showed his mother the wonderful hen.

"Hen, will you lay?" he asked the bird as he softly stroked her feathers.

It took only a few seconds for the magical hen to lay a golden egg!

Jack's mother clapped her hands with delight. "That's wonderful, Jack," she said.

Jack just smiled. "It is," he said, "but she's very tired. I'm going to make her a nest out of some straw."

The next morning when Jack woke up he went to feed the hen and saw that she had laid another golden egg. "Thank you," he said.

The hen closed her eyes and took a nap.

Each morning after that, when Jack went out to feed the hen she laid one new golden egg.

Jack and his mother lived off the golden eggs for quite some time, but as the days passed, Jack began to wonder what else he might see at the top of the beanstalk.

One fine morning he woke up early and hopped onto the

beanstalk. He climbed and climbed until he reached the top. But of course he knew better than to go right into the house of *el gigante*.

He hid in a bush by the front door until the giant woman came out with a pail to fetch some water.

Then he crept into the house and hid inside a large pot in the kitchen. It wasn't long before he heard *el gigante* cry, "Fee-fi-fo-fum. I smell the smell of a little, little man."

His wife, setting down her pail of water, looked at him with surprise. "I have no idea what you're talking about."

"I smell him, dearie, I smell him," *el gigante* insisted.

"Really?" asked the wife. "Well, it must be that little man who took your gold and the hen that lays *huevos dorados*. He's sure to be hiding in the oven." *El gigante* and his wife rushed to the oven and opened the door, but of course Jack was not there.

So *el gigante* sat down for lunch and ate enough food for ten men. Every now and then he looked around, muttering, "I thought for sure I'd smelled a fresh one." He got up to search among the pots and pans and behind the refrigerator. But luckily he didn't look inside the pot where Jack was hiding.

After finishing his lunch *el gigante* called, "Wife, wife, bring me my golden harp." So she brought it and set it down on the table in front of him.

El gigante yelled, "Sing!" And the golden harp sang beautifully.

Jack, who was peeking out from the pot, gasped. The sound was so beautiful! But when Jack looked closer he saw that the golden harp was crying golden tears. Then Jack knew that *el gigante* was as cruel to the golden harp as he'd been to the hen that laid the golden eggs. Jack thought he'd better rescue her.

When *el gigante* fell asleep his snoring drowned out the music.